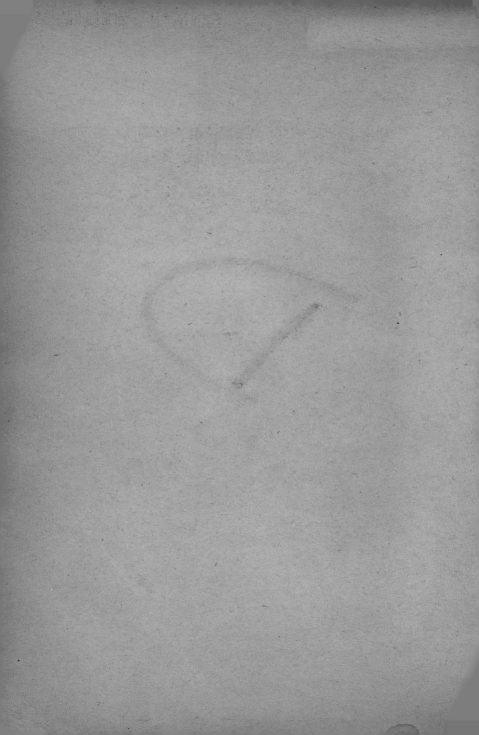

WONDER WOMAN

Power Outage

Michael Teitelbaum

Wonder Woman created by William Moulton Marston

STARSCAPE

A Tom Doherty Associates Book

New York

This is a work of fiction. All of the characters, organizations, and events portrayed in this novel are either products of the author's imagination or are used fictitiously.

WONDER WOMAN: POWER OUTAGE:
CHOOSE-YOUR-FATE ADVENTURE BOOK

Copyright © 2012 by DC Comics.
WONDER WOMAN and all related characters and elements
are trademarks of and © DC Comics.
WB SHIELD: ™ & © Warner Bros. Entertainment Inc.
[s12]

A Starscape Book
Published by Tom Doherty Associates, LLC
175 Fifth Avenue
New York, NY 10010

www.tor-forge.com

ISBN 978-0-7653-6479-1

First Edition: October 2012

Printed in the United States of America

0 9 8 7 6 5 4 3 2

How to Read This Book

You are Wonder Woman. You control your own destiny in the story you are about to read. How? At the end of each chapter, you will be asked to make a choice about what you do next. In some chapters, you will be asked to solve a puzzle that will provide a clue to help you make your choice. Occasionally you will come to a chapter that closes with "THE END." When that happens, you can go back to the beginning of the book and start again, making different choices, resulting in different outcomes.

Remember, whatever happens in the story happens because of the choices you make. So choose wisely, and get ready for the adventure of a lifetime…or *two*…or *ten*…or *twenty*!

1

YOU are Wonder Woman.

You find yourself in an intense struggle with one of your fiercest enemies—Cheetah, a feral beast in human form. Cheetah's razor-sharp claws slice at you. You must use all your agility to avoid being injured.

Reports that Cheetah was on the loose brought you to this wooded area just on the outskirts of the city. You are grateful that this battle will not affect anyone else, as it would have if you had taken on Cheetah in the heart of the city.

Cheetah leaps straight up, landing on a branch above your head. You spin and crouch, ready for the next attack. Suddenly, Cheetah is gone.

She moves more swiftly than I remember, you think. *Where did she go?*

Your question is immediately answered when Cheetah drops down from above, having jumped to a tree behind you. She knocks you to the ground and draws back her arm, ready to swipe at you again. Her beastly growl sends chills through your body, but it's her claws that are the more immediate problem.

You roll to one side, tossing Cheetah off you. You realize that taking a purely defensive posture is not going to work. You've got to go on the offensive if you are going to defeat Cheetah. But what strategy will work best?

→ If you should try to overpower Cheetah with your great strength, go to 39.

→ If you should try to use your ability to psychically talk to and calm animals, go to 34.

2

Neron has you firmly in his grasp. His powerful arms squeeze and crush you, as he did the first time you met. You feel the life draining out of your body.

I refuse to let history repeat itself. I will not die at the hands of Neron.

Mustering all your strength, you break free of Neron's grasp. Preparing to fling your Lasso of Truth once again, you suddenly feel your powers desert you.

I know now I truly must abandon this battle.

Everything around you begins to fade. You feel your life force draining. Blacking out, you tumble to the ground. When your eyes open you realize that you are back on Earth. Some unknown force has brought you here... or is all this simply happening in your mind?

Returning to your apartment, you feel very strange, and it's not only the fact that you no longer have your Amazon powers. You have lost your powers several times during this ordeal, but somehow this feels different. Are you dreaming? Is that it? Could it be possible that this is all just a bad dream?

→ If you think you are simply going to wake up from a bad dream, go to 50.

→ If you search for another explanation of all this, go to 20.

3

Ares is a brilliant military strategist. Engaging in combat with him is tricky. You realize that trying a straight-on, all-out attack will not succeed. He can meet your speed and strength with speed and strength of his own. Or he can use evasive techniques to use your own power against you. Either way, you may fail.

Flying at sub-light speed, moving with great stealth, you manage to sneak up on Ares from behind. He is still unaware of your presence. The time to strike is now!

• • • • • • • •

→ If you fling your Golden Lasso at him to force him to tell you the truth about what is going on, go to 36.

→ If you change your strategy and try to overpower Ares with your great strength, go to 16.

4

*I am an Amazon Warrior,
trained and skilled in
the ways of combat.
I fear no one—
human or demon.*
You are a master of the
sword and are fierce in combat.
You decide to put that skill to use
in your battle with Neron. Rushing
to a weapons storage area you
snatch up a huge sword, worthy
of a champion. Its sleek blade gleams
in the light. Its jewel-encrusted hilt sparkles as you
slash the weapon through the air to get a feel for its
weigh and balance.

Returning to Neron, you charge at the demon,
who has returned to his dragon form. Drawing back

your sword, you leap into the air. You bring your arm forward in a perfect arc, forming a metallic semi-circle of doom for any who may have the misfortune to meet the sword's edge.

You aim for the dragon's neck, hoping to slice its head cleanly from its body and end the terror of Neron.

But the demon is swift and clever. He instantly shape-shifts, covering his scaly dragon's skin with metal shielding. Your blade meets the dragon's neck with a deafening clang, but bounces off, having done no harm to your enemy.

Neron then creates a sword of his own from what was the dragon's tail. It dwarfs your weapon in size. He swings it toward you and you must duck quickly to avoid its enormous deadly sharp edge.

→ If you give up on the sword idea and try to use your lasso again, go to 24.

→ If you continue to battle Neron's sword with your own, go to 49.

5

Dr. Psycho! you think. *That's what Cheetah means. That would explain everything.*

Dr. Psycho is one of your most powerful and dangerous enemies. He has mind-probing psychic powers that he has used to mentally manipulate you in the past. He can control dreams and implant hallucinations into the minds of others. He can make you see and believe things that are not real.

Perhaps I didn't really lose my powers at all. Maybe Dr. Psycho controlled my mind and tricked me into thinking I lost my powers. That would answer many questions.

Should you track him down?

➜ If you should track down Dr. Psycho, go to 54.

➜ If you should seek your mother's advice, go to 33.

6

You desperately search your mind for a solution as you plunge toward Earth, gripping the bomb tightly. Suddenly, for some unknown reason, images of your home—your real Amazonian home, Paradise Island—flash in your mind.

You can't explain why, but somehow you get the feeling that everything will work out if you just return to Paradise Island. But if you do, there is still a chance that Earth and all its mortals whom you have sworn to protect will be doomed.

What should you do?

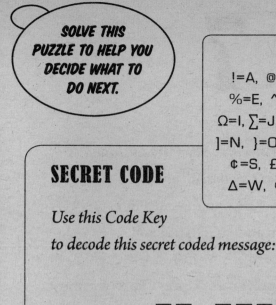

SOLVE THIS PUZZLE TO HELP YOU DECIDE WHAT TO DO NEXT.

Code Key

!=A, @=B, #=C, $=D,
%=E, ^=F, &=G, *=H,
Ω=I, ∑=J, +=K, [=L, {=M,
]=N, }=O, >=P, <=Q, ?=R,
¢=S, £=T, ¤=U, §=V,
Δ=W, ©=X, Є=Y, ◊=Z

SECRET CODE

Use this Code Key

to decode this secret coded message:

<u>&</u> <u>}</u>   <u>*</u> <u>}</u> <u>{</u> <u>%</u>

→ If you decide to disarm the bomb, go to 43.

→ If you decide to go home to Paradise Island, go to 32.

7

If I am to be the greatest warrior on Paradise Island, then I must stand my ground against all obstacles.

Again moving swiftly, you avoid the torpedoes. They speed past you and land harmlessly.

"You have successfully withstood the attack of solid weapons," Hippolyta announces. "Next you must face an assault from great sources of energy."

Without warning, searing beams of concentrated energy slice through the air heading straight for you.

➜ If you continue with this contest, go to 25.

➜ If you sense an attack coming from an even greater danger, go to 51.

8

All of this has happened before. So far, through this whole strange ordeal, each time I have let events play out as they did in the past, I have moved forward, perhaps getting closer to an explanation. Still, I can't shake this uncertain feeling...

"Are you certain that this is the right thing for me to do, Mother?" you ask.

"Of course, Diana," Hippolyta replies. "You must return to Earth and stop the danger that the mortals face. And you must remain there as its champion. It is your destiny. And the only way for you to be restored to your mortal form is with the help of the Olympian gods."

"I know you are right, Mother," you say. "I am fated to travel to Mount Olympus and be reborn at the hands of the gods there."

Still, I can't shake the feeling that this is all some kind of trick.

UNSCRAMBLE

SOLVE THIS PUZZLE TO HELP YOU CHOOSE YOUR NEXT MOVE.

Unscramble the following words and write them in the spaces. Then read down the circled column to get a clue as to where you should go next.

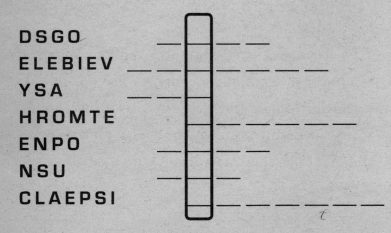

DSGO

ELEBIEV

YSA

HROMTE

ENPO

NSU

CLAEPSI

→ If you stay on course for Olympus, go to 9.

→ If you turn back to Paradise Island, go to 42.

9

Despite your unease, you realize that you must allow history to play out again. This now seems to be your destiny.

"Very well, Mother, I will go to Mount Olympus and allow the gods there to restore my mortal form," you say.

"Then prepare for your journey, Diana," Hippolyta says.

You sit quietly on a rock, listening to the gentle sound of the ocean lapping at the shoreline.

"Release your conscious thoughts," Hippolyta says in a soft, soothing voice. "Allow your mind to drift. Let me guide you."

Taking a deep breath, you begin to meditate. Thoughts race past but you let them go. Slowly you feel yourself returning to the formless void through which you have been traveling since Neron took the life from your body.

But this time, you maintain a sense of calm, seeming to know exactly how and where to move. Or maybe you are being guided by your mother's will. In either case the feeling of peace that has settled over you tells you that you have made the right choice.

Soon, the gleaming white towers of Mount Olympus appear, rising above the swirling void. You gently drift down and find yourself in a courtyard beneath the towers. There, the gods of Olympus lounge. They seem to be expecting you.

From out of nowhere a little girl approaches, carrying the most beautiful flower you have ever seen. Its petals shimmer and change color, pulsating with a soothing energy.

"Come with me," the little girl beckons, handing you the mesmerizing flower. "Follow."

. . . .

➜ If you take the flower and follow the girl, go to 31.

➜ If you grow suspicious and reject the flower, going instead to the gods who are waiting for you, go to 27.

10

You decide to head to work in your identity of Diana Prince. At work you can't stop thinking about your powers vanishing and what might be causing this strange phenomenon. After all, you have battled beings of great power from many worlds, dimensions, and universes. Your own abilities have always been a match for your adversaries. But the feeling that your own great strength, agility, combat skill, and psychic powers could blink off like a light at any moment during combat is more than a bit unsettling.

You try to have a normal day at work but you can't concentrate. Your earthly identity of Diana Prince has often come into conflict with your Amazonian identity as Wonder Woman, but this time the struggle is in your own mind.

Should you push thoughts about your failing powers aside? If not, what's your next step?

UNSCRAMBLE

SOLVE THIS PUZZLE TO HELP YOU DECIDE WHAT TO DO NEXT.

Unscramble the following words and write them in the spaces. Then read down the circled column to get a clue as to where you should look next.

BOTDU

ORYRW

LEPH

VRSEELO

ASY

RECAHS

HOWS

DREOWN

→ If you go to investigate whether or not Dr. Psycho is behind the loss of your powers, go to 5.

→ If you feel stumped and decide to return to Paradise Island to find answers to this mystery, go to 45.

11

"Will you aid me in my fight against Circe?" you ask Zeus.

"No, Diana," Zeus says gently. "We have played our part in your story and brought you back to life. You now have your powers back. The battle with Circe is yours, not ours."

"I understand," you say humbly. "And thank you."

You seek out Circe. She is waiting for you on Paradise Island.

"Now let us see who is stronger," you shout, flying at Circe and slamming into her at top speed. You drive her to the ground.

Using her sorcery, Circe conjures up an army of demons, but you tear through each one with lightning speed.

Circe is no match for you when you have your full Amazonian powers. You defeat her easily.

Circe flees into an alternate dimension to escape your fury. Just before she disappears completely, she says, "I will return to stop your quest for love, peace, and equality. You and your beliefs sicken me!"

Then she vanishes.

It feels great having all my powers back... but are they back for good?

To find out if your powers are now back for good, solve the puzzle.

HIDDEN MESSAGE

Find the word or phrase hidden in this message:

SUPERMAN ENTERS YOUR LIFE.

➔ **Go to 22.**

12

This is impossible, you think. *History cannot repeat itself. This must be some kind of illusion implanted in my mind. I will return to Paradise Island and speak with my mother.*

You return to Paradise Island and seek out your mother's counsel.

"Mother, I was engaged in battle with Ares here on Paradise Island when the illusion of being on Earth battling him was somehow placed into my mind."

"That was no illusion," Hippolyta chides you. "You truly were on Earth. You must return there and save the mortals from the threat of Ares. You cannot abandon them. You are their champion."

"But I already saved them, years ago," you point out. "I stopped Ares and the threat of his nuclear bomb. History can't repeat itself."

"You speak nonsense," Hippolyta replied. "Ares threatens Earth at this very moment and you waste your time here. It is time you faced your responsibility and saved Earth."

→ If you return to Earth and rush right into battle with Ares, go to 29.

→ If you go back to Earth and try to form a calculated battle plan, go to 44.

13

You rush toward the image of your mother. It truly is Hippolyta. She has followed you to Mount Olympus, fearing some kind of treachery, knowing you were too weak to defend yourself.

"Begone, sorceress!" Hippolyta demands, using her great power to deflect Circe's energy bolts. Then your mother turns to you.

"You must hurry, Diana. You must reach the gods so they can help you regain your solid form, be reborn, and get your powers back."

Everything around you begins to fade. Mustering your last bits of strength, you stumble to the gods, who are eagerly waiting for you.

"Come to me, Diana," Zeus says, opening his massive but welcoming arms.

Breathing a deep sigh—part relief, part exhaustion—you collapse into Zeus's arms. Then everything goes black.

You return to consciousness slowly, confused about exactly where you are. Images of Cheetah, Dr. Psycho, Neron, Circe, Hippolyta, and Zeus flash through your mind.

Your eyes flutter open slowly and you see Zeus looking down at you and smiling.

"You are back," Zeus says in a deep, commanding voice. "You are fully yourself once again—as was the case the last time I restored your life."

Looking around, you realize that you are resting comfortably on a golden bed. You once again feel the power of an Amazon warrior coursing through your veins. You sit up and look right at Zeus.

"The last time?" You repeat what Zeus has just said. "So you recall that these events have happened before?"

"Of course," Zeus replies matter-of-factly. "I am Zeus, King of the Gods, after all. Your mother may have been susceptible to the sorcery of Circe, blanking her mind of the fact that all this has happened before, but I certainly am not."

You rise to your feet, once again Wonder Woman, your body restored, your Amazon powers at their peak.

SECRET CODE

Use this Code Key to decode this secret coded message:

Code Key

!=A, @=B, #=C, $=D, %=E, ^=F, &=G, *=H, Ω=I, ∑=J, +=K, [=L, {=M,]=N, }=O, >=P, <=Q, ?=R, ¢=S, £=T, ¤=U, §=V, ∆=W, ©=X, ∈=Y, ◊=Z

‾ ‾ ‾ ‾ ‾ ‾ ‾ ‾ ‾ ‾ ‾
! £ £ ! # +   # Ω ? # %

32

WHAT IS
YOUR NEXT MOVE?

→ If you turn your power
on Circe, go to 11.

→ If you return to Earth,
go to 22.

14

You agree to enter the contest, but before it begins your mother's fears are realized. Ares attacks Paradise Island.

"You know you cannot defeat me, Diana!" Ares rages.

"I defeated you in the past and will do so again," you announce.

"You are delusional," Ares shoots back. "You have never defeated me in combat. I am Ares, God of War. No one defeats me in battle!"

Does he not remember the last time we met? you wonder. *I am the only one who realizes that I am reliving past events. Does it seem like all this is happening to him for the first time? Or is he pulling some kind of trick, trying to throw me off guard?*

As you focus on combat, Ares rushes at you, slamming into you with devastating force. You go

flying into a grove of tall palm trees, smashing them
in half. You are not hurt, due to your own Amazonian
abilities, but you must gear up for a more aggressive
offensive strategy in order to
stop Ares.

As you charge toward
Ares, fists clenched,
your Golden Lasso
at the ready, a
wave of dizziness
overcomes you.
The world starts
spinning and you
tumble to the ground, struggling to remain conscious.

The spinning stops, and
you lift yourself up off the
ground only to discover
that you are no longer on
Paradise Island. Somehow
you have been transported
back to Earth.

Looking up, you realize that you are downtown and Ares is here with his finger on the detonator of a nuclear bomb.

HIDDEN MESSAGE

SOLVE THIS PUZZLE TO HELP YOU DECIDE WHAT TO DO NEXT.

Find the hidden message in this sentence:

→ If you don't believe any of this is real and you want to return to Paradise Island, go to 12.

→ If you stay on Earth to battle Ares, go to 44.

15

You fling your lasso. But you make your move too soon. Ares is ready for you. He grabs hold of the lasso, snatching it out of the air with astonishing swiftness. Maintaining a firm grasp, Ares yanks on the lasso, pulling you toward him. In the battle that follows, you are defeated.

THE END

16

You rush at Ares, trying to overpower him with your strength.

I am the champion of the Amazons. I have defeated Ares before and I will do so again.

But Ares sees you coming and changes his own strategy. He releases his bomb, which plunges toward Earth below. You pull out your Golden Lasso, ready to fling it.

Should you fling it at Ares to learn the truth or try to lasso the bomb before it reaches Earth?

SOLVE THIS PUZZLE-->
TO LEARN WHAT YOUR NEXT
MOVE SHOULD BE.

➔ If you end up reaching Ares, go to 15.

➔ If you end up reaching the bomb, go to 59.

MAZE

Make your way through this maze to either battle Ares or go after the bomb.

17

You decide that you must confront Neron on Paradise Island, vowing to change the outcome of this confrontation. The battle begins and you find that he is just as powerful as you remembered.

You fly right at him to test his strength.

"You are no match for me, Amazon!" Neron boasts.

Using his shape-shifting ability, Neron changes from his human-looking form to that of a demon-dragon. He grows in size, dwarfing you. His body extends into a long, snake-like shape, covered in spiny scales, ending in a long tail.

Neron whips his tail at lightning speed and swats you from the sky. You tumble through the air and crash on the ground below. Neron then raises his hideous dragon head and roars, revealing a mouth full of razor-sharp teeth that now close in on you.

Somehow, despite the fact that I feel overmatched, I still find it amazing that all this has happened before. It's like I'm someone else looking down at my life unfolding—again!

Neron gives you no time to ponder this thought as his gaping dragon-jaws descend toward you.

You quickly pull out your Lasso of Truth.

Maybe if I can slip this around his neck I can control him and learn the truth.

You fling the Golden Lasso into the air. Neron is quick and clever. He instantly shifts from his dragon-shape to that of a tiny insect, easily slipping through the loop of your lasso.

You need another way to defeat him, and something clicks in your mind.

SOLVE THIS PUZZLE TO LEARN WHAT YOUR NEXT MOVE SHOULD BE.

SECRET CODE

Use this Code Key to decode this secret coded message:

Code Key

!=A, @=B, #=C, $=D,
%=E, ^=F, &=G, *=H,
Ω=I, ∑=J, +=K, [=L,
{=M,]=N, }=O, >=P,
<=Q, ?=R, ¢=S, £=T,
¤=U, §=V, Δ=W, ©=X,
€=Y, ◊=Z

$$ \underline{\&\%£} \quad \underline{!} \quad \underline{¢\,Δ\,\}\,?\,\$} $$

→ If you try to battle Neron a new way, go to 4.

→ If you try to get your lasso around him one more time, go to 61.

18

Your warrior instincts kick in and you engage the demons in battle. But you have no power and no form. You vanish into the mists of the demon dimension.

THE END

19

You return home to Earth and the mortal world, more confused than ever.

Your own problems quickly take a back seat when a report comes on the news that a terrorist has acquired a nuclear bomb and is threatening to send the world into death, destruction, and chaos by detonating it. You hurry out to see what's going on.

As Wonder Woman once again, you race downtown to find the terrorist with his finger on the detonator of a nuclear bomb. You are stunned to discover that the "terrorist" with his finger on the nuclear trigger is none other than Ares, God of War.

He must have followed me to Earth, you think, realizing that this too has happened before! Years ago, Ares had followed you to the mortal world, which he threatened to destroy in exactly the same fashion.

This is a nightmare scenario forcing you once again to relive events from long ago.

This can't be possible… can it?

→ **If you decide to battle Ares right then and there, go to 29.**

→ **If you return to Paradise Island not believing that history is actually repeating itself, go to 12.**

20

Despite all logic to the contrary, it appears that history has repeated itself. Neron has once again taken my life. As long as I fight that fact, I am doomed to walk Earth as a phantom, invisible to the mortals I encounter and even those who know me well.

You allow your mind to surrender to the truth, to the reality that you no longer walk among the living on Earth. The moment you embrace that thought, your surroundings start to shimmer with glowing light. Your feet no longer touch the ground. You find yourself floating through a formless void, neither Earth nor Paradise Island...not anywhere really at all.

Is this it? you wonder. *Am I condemned to float forever in this nowhere space?*

Up ahead, something vaguely familiar drifts into view. When you float closer, you realize that you are looking at the shores of Paradise Island, as if it is floating freely through this void.

As you approach the shoreline, you see Hippolyta waving at you and beckoning for you to come to her, to join her on the island. This whole experience has a dream-like quality.

Is it real...a trick...or actually just a dream?

What will happen if you go to your mother? Is Neron waiting for you just beyond the shore? What should you do?

. . . .

➔ If you try to get to Paradise Island to explore further, go to 48.

➔ If you begin speaking with your mother, go to 8.

21

You continue the fight, slipping free of Neron's grasp, unfurling your Lasso of Truth and flinging it at Neron. As its golden loop descends around him, you once again feel your powers desert you. You are unable to control the lasso as you normally would and Neron easily shoves it away.

This is the worst possible time for me to lose my powers, you think, hoping they will return as suddenly as they vanished.

You duck out of the way of Neron's deadly blows, relying on instinct and experience alone, knowing that you won't be able to do that forever.

"Is this the great Amazon Princess?" Neron says, scoffing at your weakness. "The champion of Paradise Island? How weak your race has grown, if you are the finest example of a warrior in combat."

Finally, one of Neron's powerful blows catches you in the head. You tumble to the ground, dizzy, shaking, feeling whatever mortal strength you possess draining from your body. Then everything goes dark.

You open your eyes and discover yourself floating in a strange limbo-like environment. No solid ground appears beneath your feet. The sky above is neither that of Earth nor Paradise Island.

Where am I? you wonder. *Am I still alive or was I unable to stop history from repeating itself? Has Neron taken my life again?*

MAZE

Make your way through this maze. Should you go to Earth or seek the help of the gods of Mount Olympus?

Go to A   **Go to B**

→ If you think this is all a bad dream and you should go to Earth, go to 50.

→ If you truly believe that **Neron** has taken your life and that only the gods of Olympus can help you, go to 20.

22

Feeling more powerful than ever, you return to Earth, where your powers remain with you permanently. You are Wonder Woman once more. You look forward to your next adventure as Earth's protector.

THE END

23

You cannot figure out whether this is some bizarre illusion, another mind trick, or whether somehow your past has come alive for you to live through once again.

And, more importantly, if you really are reliving the past, can you change the outcome this time? Can you survive another encounter with Neron and this time emerge the victor?

At the moment you see no reason to confront Neron. Why risk having him end your life again? You consider returning to Earth. You can't escape nagging thoughts that plague you.

Why can't I shake the feeling that Mother and all of Paradise Island, for that matter, are in great danger? Am I shirking my responsibility as an Amazon warrior? Am I turning my back on my true heritage? Or am I simply finding a way to survive so I can figure out what or who is behind all the recent strange events?

➔ If you decide to return to Earth, go to 28.

➔ If you stay on Paradise Island to battle Neron, go to 17.

24

How can I defeat Neron using my sword when he can change his entire body into a weapon three times the size of mine! I must try to capture him in my Golden Lasso again.

You make one more attempt to capture Neron in your lasso but he evades the golden rope once again and defeats you as he did in the past.

THE END

25

Focusing your mind, you choose a different tactic. You focus your own mental energy to meet and redirect the energy beams. The energy spreads out all around you, then veers off at a sharp angle but continues coming. Unlike the bullets, arrows, and torpedoes, the energy flows like a powerful stream of water with no end in sight.

Your senses heightened by the intense concentration required to fend off this attack, you start to get the strong feeling that an even greater danger is about to present itself. Where this danger is going to come from is unclear, but you have learned over the years to trust your instincts.

HIDDEN MESSAGE

Find the hidden message in this sentence:

➜ If you think you should stay and withstand the next attack, go to 57.

➜ If you decide to follow the sense you are getting of greater danger, go to 51.

26

Stunned by this development, you try again to penetrate Cheetah's mind and influence her. It takes all your concentration to make this second attempt, but once again you fail. Cheetah uses your lack of focus on the physical battle to overpower and defeat you.

THE END

27

You pause, spotting the gods of Olympus in the distance, calling out to you. Then, appearing to float in the sky, the image of your mother also calls to you. These powerful forces draw you and you choose to ignore the little girl, moving instead toward the Olympian gods.

Suddenly the little girl begins to change shape. She morphs into Circe, an immortal sorceress of great evil, whose goal is to destroy you. The powerful Circe hates all you value—love, peace, equality. She stands before you now, her golden crown glowing, flames leaping from her skin, her curling, flowing purple hair blowing behind her.

Everything comes clear now. All the loss of power, all the déjà vu, was caused by the sorcery of Circe. She was trying to force you to relive your life, only this time with a different ending, one that leaves you without the great powers of an Amazon warrior.

➜ If you go to the gods, go to 41.

➜ If you go to your mother, go to 13.

28

Fighting the feeling of great danger, you decide to return to Earth. But the moment you arrive all your powers vanish. You never learn why. You are rendered mortal and must remain that way for the rest of your life.

THE END

29

No time to figure out if this is real. The very existence of the human race may be at stake.

You rush toward Ares, soaring through the air, braced for battle.

"You are foolish, Diana!" Ares cackles when he spies you. "Your powers are useless against me!"

Just as you reach Ares, your powers disappear again. You plunge helplessly toward the ground below. You cannot stop Ares.

THE END

30

I can't risk my powers vanishing again, you think, staring down at the unconscious form of Cheetah. *They seem to be flickering on and off like a faulty light fixture. Best to head home and try to figure this out.*

You return home in your earthly identity of Diana Prince. Sitting in your brownstone, you ponder the sudden loss of your powers. Then a thought strikes you:

What if the very act of entering Cheetah's mind is what caused my powers to vanish temporarily? Perhaps I should not have left Cheetah. It could be that the answer lies with her. But do I dare return? What if we battle again and my powers go away like they did before?

You wrestle with this decision, knowing that you must find answers.

. . . .

→ If you go back to where you left Cheetah, go to 52.

→ If you simply head to your job, go to 10.

31

Almost unable to resist, you take the flower and follow the girl.

This is odd, you think, looking back over your shoulder. *The girl is leading me away from the Olympian gods, not toward them.*

Still, you feel compelled to follow, like this was meant to be. But when you are a short distance away from the gods, and fully out of their sight, the little girl begins to change form.

She grows in size and morphs into Circe—one of Earth's most powerful sorceresses and your worst enemy. Circe hates all you value—love, peace, equality. She stands before you, her golden crown glowing, flames leaping from her skin, her curling, flowing purple hair blowing behind her.

The truth of your whole situation comes swiftly into crystal-clear focus. Circe has been behind this whole thing—the loss of your powers, the reliving of events from your past.

"Surprise, Wonder Woman," Circe cackles. "Oh, wait...I can't call you that anymore, can I, since you are powerless. You are not even truly alive...just as I had planned."

"Why are you doing this?" you ask, but Circe ignores the question.

Summoning her sorcery, Circe unleashes a spell that casts you into a far-flung dimension, one filled with demons.

Flames rise up all around, and ghoulish, snarling demons charge at you.

→ If you try to battle the demons, go to 18.

→ If you realize that you do not have a solid form yet and can move freely between dimensions, go to 27.

32

Arriving on Paradise Island, you seek out your mother.

"I need answers, Mother," you state firmly. "My powers have been deserting me again, and this has almost cost me my life and the lives of all mortals. I need you to tell me what is going on."

"I am holding a contest, Diana," Hippolyta replies, completely ignoring your plea.

"A contest?" you ask, shocked that she is seemingly oblivious to your plight.

"I am holding a contest to find the Amazons' greatest warrior," Hippolyta explains. "But you, my daughter, are forbidden from entering."

Another piece of my past coming back again. This contest was already held. My mother already forbade me from entering it. Yet she seems not to realize any of this.

The last time this happened, I disobeyed her and entered the contest in disguise.

"Mother, this contest has already taken place," you say. "Do you have no recollection of that?"

But again, Hippolyta ignores you. "I must prepare for the contest. Be sure that you do not enter it!"

I seem destined to relive all the key events of my life, including this contest. I can't decide if I should follow the course of history and enter the contest in disguise as I did before, or try to break the pattern by doing something different.

→ **If you enter the contest in disguise, go to 37.**

→ **If you challenge your mother and enter the contest as Wonder Woman, go to 58.**

You hesitate, fearful that this is some kind of a trick or a trap. Could Dr. Psycho be toying with your mind? Is this one more step in an elaborate plot having to do with the loss of your powers?

You stare at your mother, wondering why she is sculpting a baby from clay. Is history repeating itself? Is this another child she is creating? But why would she be doing that?

MAZE

Work your way through this maze. At one exit you will reach your mother. At the other exit you will return to your earthly home.

→ If you go to your mother, go to 53.

→ If you return to your earthly home, go to 19.

34

One of your Amazonian gifts is the ability to psychically enter and calm the minds of animals. You think that maybe this will work with the human-animal hybrid that is Cheetah.

As you use your great physical strength to keep Cheetah's claws and teeth at bay, you turn your thoughts inward, clearing your mind, focusing your own psychic energy. You reach out with your thoughts, hoping you can influence Cheetah's thinking and calm her down long enough to restrain her.

Your consciousness penetrates the first layer of Cheetah's mind—the angry, confused, insane human portion, long ago suppressed by her animal side. Your psychic task is complicated by Cheetah's constant physical attacks.

Cheetah wraps her powerful arms around your shoulders.

I've got to keep her from harming me while I try to reach her inner consciousness, you think. *Not easy!*

Dropping to the ground and rolling over, you manage to shove Cheetah away from you. Using the few extra seconds this move has just bought you, your mind penetrates past her human side and engages the raw animal instincts that guide her.

At the center of Cheetah's consciousness you discover a fierce hunger and desire to destroy.

Now I must focus on that desire and try to turn it off... or at least turn it down a few notches.

Without warning and for no apparent reason, you find yourself blocked, then cast out of Cheetah's mind. Your psychic powers have never failed you before!

What is going on? you wonder.

76

WORD SEARCH

Find and circle all the following words in a word search.
Then list the remaining letters (those not circled) to
reveal a clue.

BATTLE   BEAST   STRONG   FERAL

➔ After solving the puzzle, if you think you should
continue to battle Cheetah, go to 26.

➔ If you think you should try to get away, go to 38.

35

Desperate to discover what is going on, you keep Ares in your lasso so he will reveal the truth to you, hoping to learn quickly the name of the person behind the plot and still have enough time to stop the bomb from going off.

But you are too late. Just as Ares says the name, the bomb goes off. You are defeated and Earth is doomed.

THE END

36

You toss your Lasso of Truth toward Ares. He catches the flash of movement out of the corner of his eye but your toss was too swift. The lasso descends around Ares, trapping him within its magical grasp. Anyone caught with your Golden Lasso must tell the truth.

You fly skyward, carrying Ares and his bomb with you.

"Now you will tell me why my powers keep deserting me and why it seems as if all the major events in my life are repeating themselves," you demand, knowing that he must tell you the truth. "Is this a mind illusion, some kind of time warp, a magical spell? Speak and tell me the truth!"

"It—it is a plot," Ares stammers, trying with all his will to resist telling you what you want to know. But he is unable to fight the power of your Golden Lasso. "It is all a plot by—"

At that moment, just before Ares utters the name of the person behind all the strangeness you've been going through, he releases the nuclear bomb from his grasp. The devastating weapon plunges toward Earth below.

You must now choose between learning who is behind the plot or trying to stop the bomb. What should you do?

WORD SEARCH

Find and circle all the following words in a word search. Then list the remaining letters (those not circled) to reveal a clue.

WEAPON

TOTAL

BEGIN

ARES

→ If you decide to learn who is behind the plot, go to 35.

→ If you decide to stop the bomb, go to 59.

G B O S T T

W E A P O N

O G R P T T

H I E E A B

O N S M L B

37

Choosing to follow the course of the past as it has already taken place, you enter the contest in disguise. Hiding your true identity, you take on your first opponent, another Amazon warrior. Her strength and cunning are great, but she is no match for you and you easily defeat her in combat.

Your next opponent is bigger and stronger. The hand-to-hand struggle lasts a bit longer but you are victorious in this round as well. Then you are awarded silver bracelets. If you make it through the entire contest and emerge as the greatest warrior, you will get to keep the bracelets, which will be known as Bracelets of Victory. But the competition gets tougher.

Next, your skill with these bracelets is tested. As you recall, the first time you went through this contest in the past, it took you some time to get used to the power of the bracelets and to learn how to control them. Although the events taking place now are new for everyone else, you have experienced them all before. And your memories of them are intact— including what has become instinct in the use of the silver bracelets.

And you need every bit of that instinct and skill. You next opponent fires bullets at you. You must deflect them with the bracelets. Reacting swiftly, you sense the bullets coming and position your wrists to send the deadly projectiles off in another direction.

I only hope my powers don't fail me now! you think. *If they do, I won't survive!*

After successfully deflecting bullets, you must next face a barrage of arrows fired at you from a crossbow.

Moving your arms at blinding speed, you meet the sharp point of each arrow as it zips toward you and deflect it away with your silver bracelets. Your wrists are a blur; the arrows bounce off the bracelets as if you had a shield of some kind in front of you. The barrage stops. You have successfully deflected every arrow and passed this phase of the contest, proving your worth as an Amazon warrior.

The next challenge comes in the form of torpedoes fired at you. You wonder if your bracelets are strong enough to deflect these powerful weapons.

UNSCRAMBLE

Unscramble the following words
and write them in the spaces.
Then read down the circled column
to get a clue as to what you should do.

SOLVE THIS
PUZZLE TO FIGURE
OUT YOUR NEXT
MOVE.

CDKU

ADEEV   __ __ __ __

RCNOFTON   __ __ __ __ __ __ __

ESPLE   __ __ __

ARCLBTEE __ __ __ __ __ __ __

SHCEA   __ __ __ __ __

TATAKC   __ __ __ __ __ __

→ If you decide to quit the contest, go to 60.

→ If you decide to deflect the torpedoes, go to 7.

38

You realize that something is very wrong. Your great Amazonian powers have vanished for no apparent reason. This is not a feeling you have ever experienced before. It is not something that you are the least bit comfortable with. You have come to expect those abilities to be there—always. They are second nature to you, like being Diana Prince, and their loss is a startling shock to your system.

I can't understand why I'm unable to penetrate Cheetah's mind, you think.

The psychic approach having failed, you refocus your mind on the physical battle at hand. Slipping around behind Cheetah, you pin her arms to her sides.

At least I can keep her restrained for the moment, you think. *But then what?*

Cheetah snarls, her fury increasing as she writhes wildly, trying to free herself from your vise-like grip. You didn't think it was possible for her to descend any lower into a feral state, but her imprisonment in your powerful arms sends her into an even deeper animal frenzy.

Then, once again, inexplicably, your powers leave you. This time, it's your great Amazonian strength that disappears.

Instantly sensing this, Cheetah thrusts her arms out to the side, breaking free of your grasp.

This is more serious than I first thought, you realize, not taking the time to bother thinking about why your powers suddenly disappeared. *Without my strength, I'm no match for Cheetah!*

Cheetah spins around to face you, her eyes blazing red with rage. You duck and spin out of the way as she swipes at you with her razor-sharp claws, barely avoiding their deadly intent.

Tiring of the cat and mouse game, Cheetah leaps right at you, knocking you down. She lands on you with the full force of her weight, pinning you to the ground.

You are helpless.

Am I fated to die like this, at the hands of this raging beast, my Amazonian powers having betrayed me?

Suddenly you feel a great rush of strength. Energy surges through your veins. Your powers have returned as abruptly and inexplicably as they deserted you.

With a powerful thrust, you shove Cheetah off you. She slams into a wall and slumps to the ground, unconscious.

→ If you are worried that your powers will disappear again during your fight with Cheetah and want to try and figure out what's going on, go to 30.

→ If you try to revive Cheetah to question her, go to 52.

39

It's time to attack, and you decide that your great Amazonian strength offers you the best chance to defeat Cheetah. You grab her, but find that her own strength, though not as great as yours, coupled with her animal ferocity, poses a challenge.

You manage to wrestle Cheetah to the ground and jump onto her. You prepare to end this struggle and finish her off when suddenly a wave of weakness overcomes you. You feel your strength vanishing as if someone had drained all the exceptional power from your body.

Cheetah's animal instincts help her sense this change. She now sees you as vulnerable prey. Her eyes open wide and she flings you from her. You smash into a thick tree trunk and everything goes dark.

THE END

40

You decide to
use all the tools
at your disposal.
You unfurl your
Golden Lasso.

Perhaps I can take
care of two problems at
once, you think, prepar-
ing to throw the
Golden Lasso.
Not only can I restrain
Ares, but my Golden Lasso
will force him to tell the truth. I may
finally get some answers about my past
and present and how they seem to be colliding.

With great skill, you spin and fling your
Lasso of Truth at Ares.

But Ares is a swift warrior. He sees your lasso coming and ducks out of the way.

→ If you immediately fling your lasso at Ares again, go to 15.

→ If you retreat and approach Ares from another angle before flinging your lasso again, go to 36.

41

You move toward the gods, knowing that this is what your mother intended for you, realizing that this is the only way to restore your human form and your Amazonian powers.

Circe, having revealed herself, pursues you.

"I command you to obey me and follow me to the demon dimension where you will meet your final doom!" she shouts.

You ignore her and continue drifting toward the gods.

"You dare defy me!" Circe bellows. "You who have lost all your power. It is my sorcery that has brought you to your knees. I sent Cheetah and controlled Dr. Psycho. I have drawn your powers away, though I must admit your will is strong, so strong that each time your powers returned.

"I sent Neron to slay you once again. Only this time you will remain dead. This time I will defeat you. This time I will be the more powerful force. Behold my power!"

Furious that you won't obey her, even in your weakened state, Circe fires powerful energy bolts at you from her hands. You are too weak to stop the bolts.

→ If you stand your ground and fight Circe, go to 56.

→ If you try to run to your mother, go to 13.

MAZE *Navigate the maze.*

42

This still feels like a trick. Why am I being forced to relive history? Is someone leading me into a trap from which there is no return? I just don't trust the way things are going. It feels like someone has laid out a path step by step for me, and I'm following it blindly, just because events played out this way once before.

"I don't think I will go to Mount Olympus," you tell your mother, mostly to see what her reaction will be. If she is somehow being controlled as part of a plan meant to do you harm, you might be able to tell from her response.

"Then you will cease to exist, my child," Hippolyta replies calmly. "Your consciousness will begin to fade, and once it blinks out, there will be no way to bring you back. I will not be able to do it, nor will the Olympian gods. You must journey to Olympus now, while you still can; otherwise all hope is lost. I will have lost my daughter forever and the mortals of Earth will have lost their champion."

You sense no deceit in your mother's tone. And as she completes her statement, the image of your mother standing before you and, in fact, of Paradise Island itself begins to fade from your view. You feel yourself leaving, once again being pulled into the great formless void.

What should you do?

HIDDEN MESSAGE

Find the message hidden in this sentence:

PICK UP THE PHONE AND JINGLE A VET.

➜ If you decide to stay, go to 55.

➜ If you leave and go to Olympus, go to 9.

43

You tear open the door to the inner workings of the bomb and start ripping wires out. At least if you plunge to your doom, you figure, the bomb will fall harmlessly to the ground and only you will perish, but the planet will be safe.

Seconds before you hit the ground, your powers suddenly return, just as inexplicably as they vanished. Having the ability to fly and your great strength back once again, you guide the bomb safely and gently to Earth.

There is no sign of Ares, and you arrange for a team of nuclear scientists to dismantle the bomb safely and dispose of the nuclear material. But this on-and-off loss of your powers has now almost cost you your life several times, and you are no closer to understanding it.

I must return to Paradise Island and find some answers!

You journey once again to your Amazonian home.

➜ If you ask your mother what she knows about the mystery, go to 32.

➜ If you search for answers elsewhere on Paradise Island, go to 37.

44

You return to Earth, more confused than ever.

Am I the only one who realizes that history is repeating itself? No time to worry about that now. I must treat the threat from Ares as real.

Returning downtown, you discover that Ares still stands with his finger on the trigger of a nuclear bomb. It appears as if no time has passed here since you transported to Paradise Island.

You must choose your next offensive move carefully. Ares is an extremely powerful, dangerous, and clever foe. And the fact that he possesses a nuclear bomb puts the entire planet in jeopardy, so you are fighting not just for your own survival but for the survival of the human race—the race, as your mother pointed out, you have sworn to protect and defend.

Although you possess great Amazonian strength, Ares is also supernaturally strong, and you are not sure that you can defeat him with your own strength alone. You ponder several strategies.

→ If you decide to capture Ares with your Lasso of Truth to force him to tell you the truth, go to 40.

→ If you decide to fly at sub-light speed and surprise Ares with a sneak attack, go to 3.

45

You return to your true home—
Paradise Island. It is the
home of the immortal
Amazons, the race
of warrior women
created by the goddess
Aphrodite and the
Olympian gods
to stop Ares,
God of War.

You know
that you will
be safe from
whatever force has
been causing you to
lose your powers here,
since Paradise Island is

hidden from the mortal world on Earth by a dense cloud formation and a mystical cloak of invisibility.

When you arrive, you seek out your mother, Hippolyta, Queen of the Amazon Warriors, hoping to get advice from her. Moving through the lush, tropical beauty of Paradise Island, you pass rushing waterfalls dropping into calm pools of water, and grand white palaces rising from the smooth rocks. Tall, graceful palm trees sway gently in the warm breeze. Amazon warriors rest among the magnificent natural wonder of the island that is truly a slice of paradise.

You spot your mother in the distance but are confused by what you see. Hippolyta appears to be working with a lump of clay, shaping and molding the pliable material with her hands.

What is she making? you think.

Approaching slowly, you are shocked and stunned to discover that your mother is sculpting a baby from clay.

This is how I came into being in the first place, sculpted from clay and brought to life by Hippolyta!

You are confused. What are you witnessing—the past reliving itself? A hallucination implanted by Dr. Psycho? A different kind of mind trick?

→ If you hesitate, thinking this might be some kind of mind-control trick, go to 33.

→ If you rush to your mother to find out what is going on, go to 53.

46

You battle on, struggling to gain the upper hand in the sword contest. But you continue to lose ground.

Should I flee? Should I save myself now or continue the fight, hoping to stop the threat of Neron once and for all?

Neron continues to grow stronger and you feel yourself weakening. History is about to repeat itself. Neron is going to beat you if you stay in this fight.

SOLVE THIS PUZZLE TO DISCOVER WHAT YOU SHOULD DO NEXT.

WORD SEARCH

Find and circle all the following words in a word search. Then list the remaining letters (those not circled) to reveal a clue.

DIANA   DEFEAT   NERON   STOP

D	I	A	N	A	S
D	E	F	E	A	T
C	O	N	R	T	O
I	N	U	O	E	P
F	I	G	N	H	T

→ If you should stop the fight and leave Paradise Island, go to 2.

→ If you feel compelled to continue, hoping to find a reserve of strength, go to 21.

47

You decide to question Dr. Psycho, figuring that you have nothing to lose. If this is indeed a dead end, you might as well find out right now while you are here anyway.

The guards unlock the door to the room holding Dr. Psycho and then they leave you alone with him.

"How long have you been here?" you ask, starting off with a simple question.

Dr. Psycho mumbles something underneath his breath. You lean in close to try to understand him. As you do, he manages to catch one corner of the psychic-dampening headband on the point of your tiara. Jerking his head to the side, he rips the headband off.

Released from the headband's power, Dr. Psycho is free to use his considerable mental abilities against you. He plants the idea in your mind that you should return to your life and forget he ever existed. You not only completely forget him but also lose all memory of the incidents of losing your powers.

THE END

48

You decide to try to reach your mother on Paradise Island. Floating weightlessly through the void, you attempt to guide yourself to the shoreline. After what feels like hours, you finally hover above the shore. Below, your mother still waves at you.

I really hope I'm not walking right into a trap, you think.

You curl your body into a ball and drop to the sands of Paradise Island. Regaining your fully-weighted form, you jump to your feet ready to continue your battle with Neron. But there is no sign of the demon prince.

"Mother!" you cry, as Hippolyta rushes to your side. "What is going on?"

"Your mortal form has been slain by Neron," Hippolyta explains. "But you can be given new life by the gods on Mount Olympus."

"They will do that for me again?" you ask, recalling that the Olympian gods restored your life the first time Neron defeated you.

"Your work on Earth is not finished, Diana," Hippolyta replies. "You must now journey to Olympus and be brought back to life, so you can resume your role as champion to the mortals of Earth."

→ If you follow your mother's advice and continue on your journey to Mount Olympus, go to 8.

→ If you stay on Paradise Island, go to 42.

49

Trusting in your great skill and swordsmanship, you engage Neron, meeting a swipe from his giant sword with your own. The enormous impact sends you stumbling backwards, but you manage to keep your feet.

You go on the offensive again, but your powerful blows land harmlessly on his body, which is now coated with steel armor.

Neron fights back and begins to overpower you. The terrifying sense of déjà vu that has plagued you recently is in full force. This has all happened before. You have battled Neron and he has defeated you, taking your life. It appears that this is about to happen again!

➔ If you should fight on, thinking that history can't repeat itself, go to 46.

➔ If you should flee now to save your life, go to 2.

50

Your mind races for answers. You focus on returning to Earth and suddenly find yourself at home in your apartment. You head to work as Diana Prince.

"Good morning, Stacy," you say to one of your co-workers, a person you've known for years.

She acts as if you aren't even in the room.

Well, that's odd.

You run into another co-worker.

"Hello, Fred," you say, smiling.

Again, someone you have known for quite a while walks right past you.

Does anybody know I'm here?

"Hello!" you shout. No one reacts.

Stepping up to a desk, you swipe your hand at a book, trying to knock it onto the floor, but your hand passes right through the book.

You run outside and start talking to people on the street. Again, no one takes any notice of you.

It's like I'm not really here.

Then it dawns on you.

I'm not really here, am I? Neron has taken my life again. That is the only logical explanation. Or is it?

→ If you truly believe that Neron has taken your life and that only the gods of Olympus can help you, go to 20.

→ If you try to get back to Paradise Island to continue the fight with Neron, go to 48.

51

I must stay and find out why I have this impending sense of doom.

You don't have long to wait. An imposing figure rises up in front of you. It has the shape of a human man, but continues to grow in size, dwarfing your form, gazing down at you with contempt.

"I am Neron, Demon Prince, Ruler of Hell," the towering figure before you announces. "I am here to destroy the one that mortals call Wonder Woman."

Neron! I have faced him before, although, like everyone else, he does not recall those events from the past. Only I do. He took my life the last time we met. I was brought back to life by the Olympian gods. I don't wish to go through that again.

Neron possesses enormous mystical powers, can change his size and shape, and is a master of lies and deception.

Should you confront him or retreat?

→ If you retreat, go to 23.

→ If you confront him, go to 17.

52

You slowly, carefully approach the unconscious form of Cheetah. You pause for a second, checking to make sure your powers are in place. Your mind races, fearful that your great abilities will desert you again when you need them most. Still, you need to figure out what is going on and why Cheetah had suddenly reappeared after many years.

Grabbing Cheetah's shoulders, you shake her slightly. She moans, then shakes her head. As her vision clears, Cheetah spots you leaning over her. Her fury rises again, but you are prepared. Using your great strength, you hold her down.

"Why are you back?" you ask firmly. "And what do you know about why my powers keep vanishing?"

Cheetah snarls at you, unleashing a feral growl.

Once again, you reach out psychically and enter Cheetah's mind. This time you navigate past the outer

layers of enraged humanity and probe to the very center of her animal being. But you find no answers awaiting. Changing strategies, you reach out with your mind and implant the suggestion to calm down, to stop resisting.

Cheetah struggles against this command at first, but then you feel her rage ease off.

"Tell me what you know about my powers!" you demand again.

Cheetah hisses at you, but with less fury. Through the animal sounds she makes, you think you can make out a single clear word.

Did she just say "psycho"?

→ **If you think that Cheetah is just babbling nonsense, go to 10.**

→ **If you think you have figured out what Cheetah meant by "psycho," go to 5.**

53

This is crazy! you think. *She's my mother. What am I afraid of?*

You hurry to your mother's side. She doesn't seem the least bit surprised to see you. She continues to work with the clay, shaping a child.

"Mother, what are you doing?" you ask.

"It is time, Diana," Hippolyta replies, ignoring your question.

"Time? Time for what?" you ask, growing more puzzled by the minute.

"Why, the contest, of course," Hippolyta explains. "The contest to find the greatest warrior on Paradise Island. We have discovered that Ares is planning to start a war."

Again you are stunned. Long ago, you won the contest and proved your worth as a great warrior. You received your Golden Lasso and your silver bracelets as a reward for your victory, left Paradise Island and became Wonder Woman.

Why does history appear to be repeating itself? First Hippolyta is sculpting you as a child from clay. Now she wants you to go through your battle with Ares again. This makes no sense.

Still, you do not want to go against the wishes of your mother. She is wise and she is also your queen. Conflict rages within you. Something about this whole situation just feels wrong.

You ponder what to do next.

➜ If you decide to enter the contest, go to 14.

➜ If you return home to Earth sensing that something is just not right, go to 19.

54

Using your contacts and inside information, you search around and check law enforcement databases.

It doesn't take you long to discover the whereabouts of Dr. Psycho. He's being held in a top-secret, maximum security metahuman detention center, where prisoners with powers beyond those of normal humans are securely kept.

As Wonder Woman, you arrange to see Dr. Psycho. Arriving at the facility, you are not surprised to see that from the outside it looks like any other prison.

But upon entering, you discover just how special a place this is.

The guards lead you through thick steel doors that slam shut behind you with a deep, imposing clang. Following the guards down a long, narrow hallway, you eventually come to a tiny room. Peering through a thick reinforced window in the door leading into the room, you spot Dr. Psycho.

He is bound and shackled, limiting his physical movements. But in order to ensure that he doesn't escape from the facility, Dr. Psycho is also hooked up to a headband that dampens his psychic powers.

This device, unique to this metahuman detention center, prevents Dr. Psycho from using his powers to create illusions in the minds of others. If it were not in place, he could simply implant the idea in the minds of the guards to let him walk free. The headband device keeps Dr. Psycho from using his mental abilities.

How could he have reached into my mind? you wonder. *He's got that psychic-dampening headband on. Maybe I'm chasing a dead-end lead.*

What should you do next?

> **SOLVE THIS PUZZLE TO HELP YOU DECIDE WHAT TO DO NEXT.**

SECRET CODE

Code Key

!=A, @=B, #=C, $=D, %=E, ^=F, &=G,
*=H, Ω=I, ∑=J, +=K, [=L, {=M,]=N, }=O,
>=P, <=Q, ?=R, ¢=S, £=T, ¤=U, §=V,
Δ=W, ©=X, €=Y, ◊=Z

Use this Code Key to decode this secret coded message:

_ _ _ _ _ _ _ _

> ! ? ! $ Ω ¢ %

• • • • • • •

→ If you decide that Dr. Psycho can't have been respon-
sible for your power loss and decide to go to Paradise
Island, go to 45.

→ If you decide to question Dr. Psycho, go to 47.

55

You stubbornly refuse to leave. As you stand before your mother, you feel your life force draining from you. A few moments later your consciousness fades and disappears.

THE END

56

*I am already separated from my body. I'm betting that
without my solid mortal form, Circe's energy bolts won't
hurt me.*

You decide to stand your ground. Circe fires her
energy bolts, but as you suspected, they pass harmlessly through you. Without your mortal form, you
cannot be hurt by them. But time is running out. You
begin to feel weak. You cannot exist in this limbo
form for much longer.

Hippolyta rushes to your side.

"Hurry, Diana," she says urgently, cradling you in
her arms. "You must go to the Olympian gods and
allow them to restore you."

Everything around you begins to fade. Mustering
your last bits of strength, you stumble to the gods,
who are eagerly waiting for you.

"Come to me, child," Zeus says, opening his massive but welcoming arms.

Breathing a deep sigh—part relief, part exhaustion—you collapse into Zeus's arms. Then everything goes black.

You return to consciousness slowly, confused about exactly where you are. Images of Cheetah, Dr. Psycho, Neron, Circe, Hippolyta, and Zeus flash through your mind.

Your eyes flutter open slowly and you see Zeus looking down at you and smiling.

"You are back, child," Zeus says in a deep, commanding voice. "You are fully yourself once again—as was the case the last time I restored your life."

Looking around, you realize that you are resting comfortably on a golden bed. You once again feel the power of an Amazon warrior coursing through your veins. You sit up and look right at Zeus.

"The last time?" You repeat what Zeus has just said. "So you recall that these events have happened before?"

"Of course," Zeus replies matter-of-factly. "I am Zeus, King of the Gods, after all. Your mother may have been susceptible to the sorcery of Circe, blanking her mind of the fact that all this has happened before, but I certainly am not."

You rise to your feet, once again Wonder Woman, your body restored, you Amazon powers at their peak. History did repeat itself, but once again you are strong, you are Wonder Woman. Do you attack Circe alone or try to enlist the gods to help you?

. . . .

→ If you ask the gods to help you, go to 11.

→ If you attack Circe, go to 22.

57

You stand your ground. It is important to you to finish this challenge and win the contest, proving yourself to be the Amazons' greatest warrior. The searing beams of laser energy give way to jagged bolts of lightning.

Fearful that your body will not be able to re-direct the lightning, you once again return to your speed, avoiding the bolts which slam harmlessly into the ground.

You have passed every test.

"Despite my protests, you have entered and won the contest, Diana," Hippolyta says. "You are truly the champion of Paradise Island. You may now have the Bracelets of Victory and the Golden Lasso of Truth."

You are relieved to have won the contest, as you did the first time you lived through these events. But you can't shake the feeling that some great danger awaits, that someone is out to do you harm. You ponder your next decision, unsure whether you should return to Earth or explore your sense of a greater danger here on Paradise Island.

MAZE

SOLVE THIS PUZZLE TO HELP YOU DISCOVER WHO IS BEHIND THE DANGER YOU SENSE.

Navigate the maze to either go back to Earth or confront the danger.

go to
A

go to
B

• • • • • • • •

→ If you decide to go back to Earth, go to 28.

→ If you pursue the greater danger, go to 51.

58

You decide to challenge your mother and participate in the contest as Wonder Woman.

"I am a worthy warrior and a proud Amazon," you state defiantly. "I see no reason why I should not take part in the contest to find Paradise Island's greatest warrior."

This is all so familiar, you think, having had this exact conversation with your mother before. You know what she is going to say before she says it. But she does not seem to remember any of this happening before.

"I forbid you from entering the contest," Hippolyta says. You are my daughter and an Amazonian princess."

Your will is strong and your mother cannot stop you. You prepare for a series of attacks. First a barrage of bullets comes buzzing toward you. Using your speed and cunning, you manuever out of their way.

Next comes a volley of arrows fired from cross-bows. Again, you manage to avoid the attack.

Then a series of torpedoes comes rocketing at you. You are not certain what to do.

→ If you decide to quit and return to Earth, go to 28.

→ If you stand your ground, go to 7.

59

You race after the bomb, intent on stopping it before it destroys Earth. You pull out your Golden Lasso, hoping you can somehow capture the bomb and guide it into the sun, where it can detonate harmlessly. But when you reach the plunging bomb, your powers once again disappear. You have lost the power of flight and you plunge helplessly toward Earth, holding tightly to the bomb.

→ If you try to recall what helped you regain your powers the last time they vanished, go to 6.

→ If you try to disarm the bomb, go to 43.

60

Your bracelets can deflect any object hurtling toward you. But you're not sure if they can handle the impact of an exploding weapon. You step aside, letting the torpedoes zoom past you. Then you quit the contest, still keeping your identity a secret.

You leave Paradise Island with all the mysteries unsolved. You never learn why history is repeating itself and you never discover why you continue to lose your powers.

The moment you leave Paradise Island and return to Earth, all your powers vanish, and they never return. You are rendered mortal for the remainder of your life.

THE END

61

You decide to take your chances, by tossing your lasso at him *again*. At least if you capture him within your golden rope, you can force him to reveal the truth. But Neron evades your lasso once again, reverts to his dragon form, and defeats you.

THE END

Answers

6

GO HOME

8

OLYMPUS
gods, believe, say, mother, open, sun, special

10

DR. PSYCHO
doubt, worry, help, resolve, say, search, show, wonder

11

suPERMAN ENTers your life
(PERMANENT)

13

ATTACK CIRCE

14

bring BACK TOE ART, Hippie
(BACK TO EARTH)

16

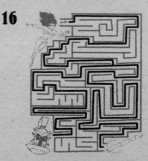

17

GET A SWORD

21

25

sELECT RICk to help
(ELECTRIC)

33

34
LOST POWERS

B	E	A	S	T
A	L	O	T	L
T	S	T	R	A
T	P	O	O	R
L	W	E	N	E
E	R	S	G	F

36
GO STOP THE BOMB

G	B	O	S	T	T
W	E	A	P	O	N
O	G	R	P	T	T
H	I	E	E	A	B
O	N	S	M	L	B

37
DEFLECT
duck, evade, conront, sleep, bracelet, chase, attack

41

42
pick up the phone and jingLE A VEt. (LEAVE)

46
CONTINUE FIGHT

D	I	A	N	A	S
D	E	F	E	A	T
C	O	N	R	T	O
I	N	U	O	E	P
F	I	G	N	H	T

54
PARADISE

57

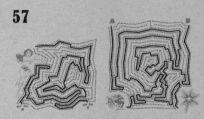

Congratulations! You've captured the super-villains by following this path: 1, 34, 38, 30, 52, 10, 5, 54, 45, 33, 53, 14, 12, 44, 40, 36, 59, 6, 43, 32, 37, 7, 25, 57, 51, 23, 17, 4, 49, 46, 2, 50, 20, 48, 8, 9, 31, 27, 41, 56, 11, 22